Jake

and His Cousin Sidney

Jake's Dad

This Jake book
belongs to

. . . .

For Norman, my friend — and my accountant,
with love

First published 1994 by Macmillan Children's
Books, an imprint of Macmillan Publishers Limited.

First U.S. edition 2002

Library of Congress Cataloging-in-Publication Data

James, Simon, date.
Jake and his cousin Sidney /
Simon James. — 1st U.S. ed.
p.   cm.
Summary: When Jake tries to give his baby
cousin Sidney a bath, a wet disaster ensues.
ISBN 0-7636-1801-2
[1. Baths — Fiction. 2. Behavior — Fiction.
3. Cousins — Fiction. 4. Babies — Fiction.] I. Title.
PZ7.J1544 Jak 2002
[E] — dc21   2001058210

10 9 8 7 6 5 4 3 2 1

Printed in Hong Kong

This book was typeset in Usherwood Book.
The illustrations were done in watercolor and ink.

Candlewick Press
2067 Massachusetts Avenue
Cambridge, Massachusetts 02140

visit us at www.candlewick.com

With warm thanks to Sian for photography

Jake
and His Cousin
Sidney

Simon James

CANDLEWICK PRESS
CAMBRIDGE, MASSACHUSETTS

Jake was difficult.
Jake was a problem.
And Jake didn't like babies. All they
seemed to do was cry and smell something
awful. So you can imagine how Jake felt
one day when he had to take care
of his cousin Sidney.

Jake did his best.
He fed Sidney his baby food.
He even changed Sidney's diaper.
Then Jake's mother said
it was time for Sidney's bath.

Jake carried Sidney upstairs to the bathroom
and turned on the faucets.
The bathtub always took such a long time to fill.
So Jake thought he'd go to his room
and read for a while.
Sidney waited.

And he waited.

In fact, it was quite some time

before Jake remembered Sidney's bath.

Jake ran out of his bedroom toward the

bathroom door . . .

. . . only to find Sidney floating out on the crest of a gigantic wave.

"Be brave, Sidney!" called Jake, as he jumped onboard . . .

and rode the rapids downstairs to the hall.

Meanwhile, in the living room, Jake's father
began to wonder what the loud slurping noise
was in the hallway.
He got up from his chair and walked
toward the door.

Jake and Sidney, meanwhile, were beginning to wonder just how much MORE water would fill the hall.

Fortunately, Jake's father opened the living room door just in time.
"Hooray!" said Jake.

At that moment, Jake's sister came home
from her Brownies meeting. She'd just
reached the front door when suddenly . . .

out burst her mother, her
father, several pieces of furniture,
and at the top of a huge tidal
wave, Jake and his cousin Sidney.
Jake's sister was drenched.

Jake's parents stood helplessly
as their beautiful home, now
filled to the brim with water,
slowly lifted up from the ground
and started to float down the road.

That night Jake's father had to check the whole family into the local hotel. He made sure that Jake and Sidney shared a room by themselves.

But Jake didn't mind taking care of his brave little cousin.
And Sidney certainly didn't cry.
He knew . . .

. . . he'd grow up to be just like Jake.

love from
Jake and Sidney

SIMON JAMES is the author-illustrator of many acclaimed books for
children, including *The Day Jake Vacuumed, Jake and the Babysitter,
Jake and His Cousin Sidney, Days Like This, The Wild Woods,* and
Leon and Bob, which was named a *New York Times Book Review*
Best Illustrated Children's Book of the Year.